Jafta's Mother

Story by Hugh Lewin
Pictures by Lisa Kopper

Carolrhoda Books, Inc. / Minneapolis

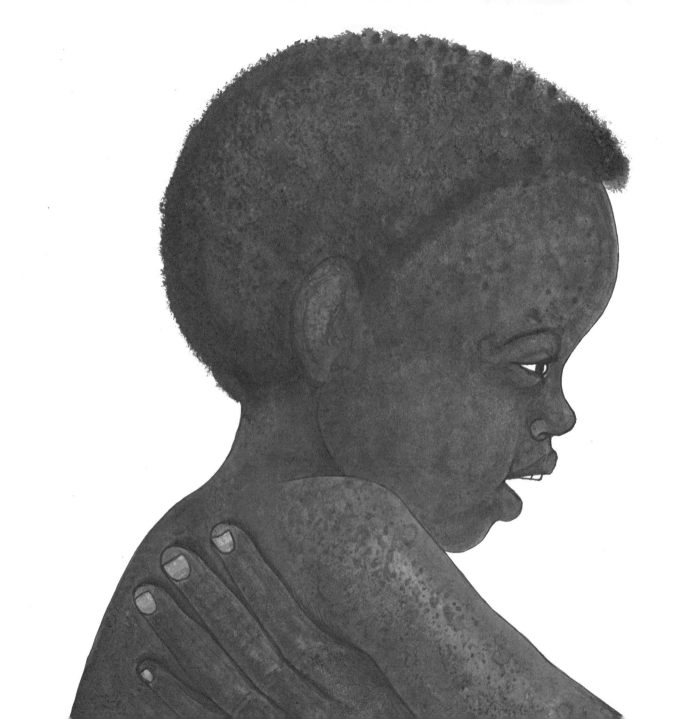

I would like you, said Jafta, to meet my mother.
There is nobody I know quite like my mother.

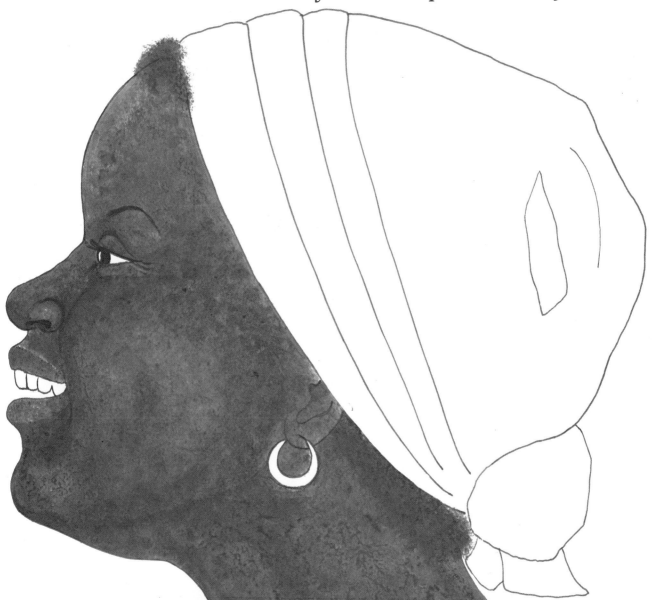

My mother is like the earth—
full of goodness, warm and brown and strong.

My mother is like the sun rising
in the early morning,
lighting up the dark corners
and gently coaxing us awake.
She prods the fire into life
and soon everywhere is filled
with the smoky smell of food,
bringing rumbles to my tummy
and making me want to get up.

As the sun starts its day
and the flowers burst open
to turn and follow it
across the sky,
I think of my mother.

Like the sky, she's always there.
You can always look up
and see her.

At midday when the sun is high and strongest,
she shades and comforts us,
like the willows on the bank of the river.

Or when the day has become too hot and stuffy,
she cools us as the rain does
when it turns the dust-bowls into rippling puddles,
washing out the grass and making it green again.

She doesn't often complain,
even in the bad times.

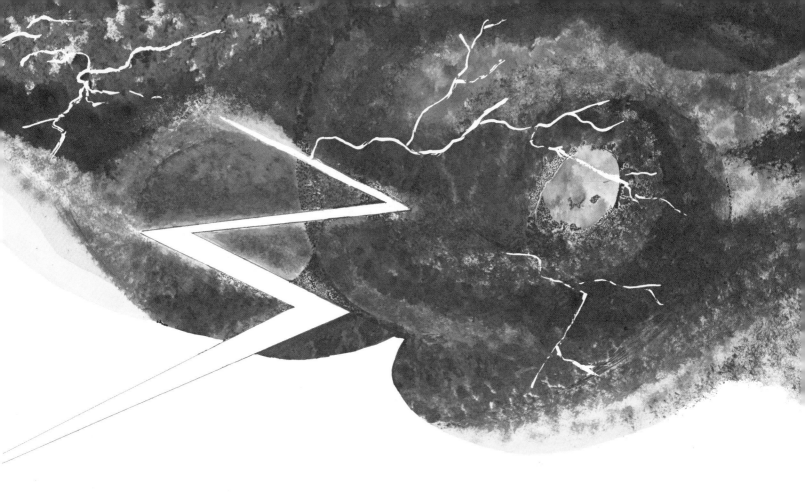

But beware! If she finds you cheating at a game,
or teasing your younger sisters,
she can sound like thunder in the afternoon
and her eyes will flash
like the lightning out of the dark clouds.

My mother doesn't often storm, said Jafta,
and it's much nicer when she sings.
She sings to us
as she cooks the evening meal.
If you've heard a hoopoe call
across the mealies,
you've heard my mother sing.

After supper it's time for the stories. Somehow,
said Jafta, I think I almost love my mother best then–

after the food and the hurrying, when the sun's going down and everything's quieter and cooler.

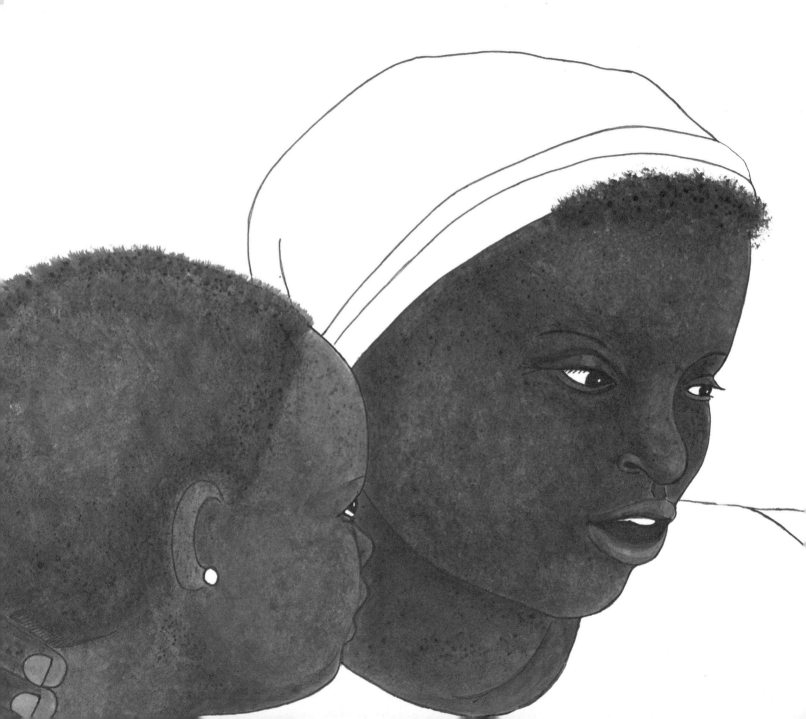

Then she hugs us 'round her and chases away our sadnesses.
We talk about today, and yesterday,
and especially tomorrow.

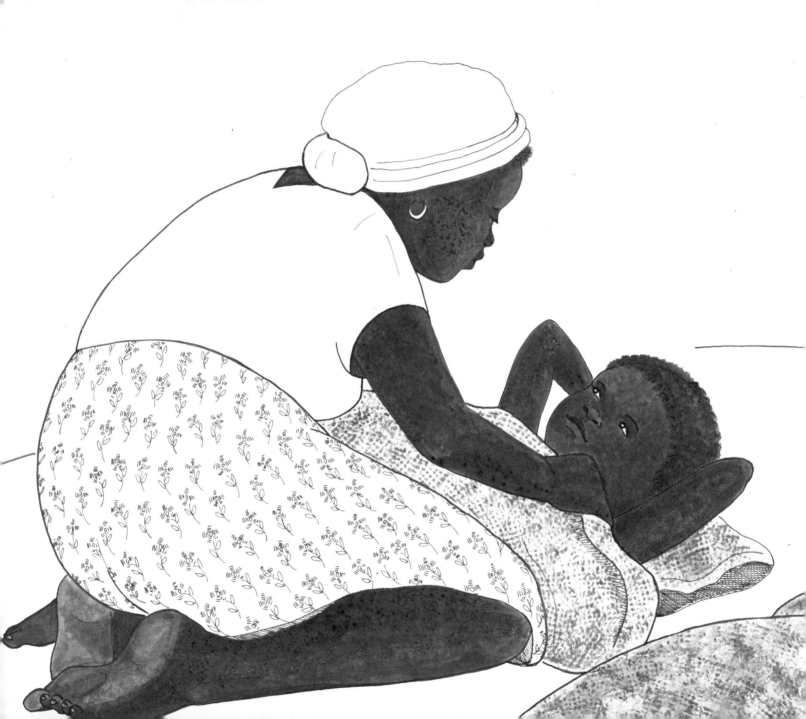

Then, as the blanket of night
spreads out over the world,
with a bright moon above,
my mother wraps us up carefully
and with a kiss and goodnight
puts us to sleep.

There are some words in this story that might be new to you. A hoopoe is a colorful pinkish-brown bird common in South Africa. Its name derives from its deep, haunting call of "hoop-hoop . . . hoop-hoop." Mealies, from the Afrikaans "mielies," is maize, or corn-on-the-cob.

This book is available in two editions:
Library binding by Carolrhoda Books, Inc.
Soft cover by First Avenue Editions
241 First Avenue North
Minneapolis, Minnesota 55401

LIBRARY OF CONGRESS CATALOGING-IN-PUBLICATION DATA

Lewin, Hugh.
   Jafta's mother.

   Originally published as: Jafta–my mother.
   Summary: A little boy living in an African village
describes his mother and the love he feels for her.
   [1. Mothers-Fiction. 2. Africa-Social life and customs]
I. Kopper, Lisa, ill. II. Title.
PZ7.L58418Jai   1983   [E]   82-12863
ISBN 0-87614-208-0 (lib. bdg.)
ISBN 0-87614-495-4 (pbk.)

This edition first published in 1983 by Carolrhoda Books, Inc.
Original edition published in 1981 by Evans Brothers Limited,
London, England, under the title JAFTA–MY MOTHER.
Text copyright © 1981 by Hugh Lewin.
Illustrations copyright © 1981 by Lisa Kopper.
All rights reserved.

Manufactured in the United States of America

6   7   8   9   10   92   91